PYEWACKET

Pyewacket

BY *ROSEMARY WEIR*

ILLUSTRATED BY CHARLES PICKARD

ABELARD-SCHUMAN

London . New York . Toronto

By the same author:

Albert the Dragon
Further Adventures of Albert the Dragon
The Smallest Dog on Earth
Mike's Gang
The Boy From Nowhere

© Rosemary Weir 1967
First published 1967
L.C.C.C. No. 67–19581

London Abelard-Schuman Limited, 8 King Street, WC2
New York Abelard-Schuman Limited, 6 West 57 Street
Toronto Abelard-Schuman Canada Limited, 896 Queen Street West

CONTENTS

I *A Street of Cats*

The street was short and narrow, hardly more than a lane. At the end by the Market Square, it was tidy and respectable, but it got rapidly shabbier until at the end by the canal it really wasn't a nice street at all. It was called Pig Lane, and there were only seven houses, all on the same side of the road. On the other side there was a high fence, and behind the fence was a vacant lot overgrown with coarse grass and brambles. The people of the town dumped rubbish there; old iron bedsteads and broken-down bicycles and even worn-out cars. It made a lovely place for the children to play, but the more respectable people said it was a disgrace and why wasn't something done about it?

One day a factory was to be built there, and it said so on a large, weather-beaten sign. But no one knew when that day would come, and in the meantime the children played, and dogs raced and barked and dug holes. But when darkness fell and the dogs and children went home, the vacant lot was taken over by the cats.

Every house in Pig Lane had its cat. In the best house, at the Market Square end, lived a Siamese called Chi Ki. His owners kept a ladies' hair-dressing establishment. They were out all day, which made it very lonely for Chi Ki, who was left shut up indoors.

At No. 2 there was a marmalade tom cat whose name was Ginger. Two old ladies owned him and loved him a great deal more than he loved them. Ginger was very independent and had a poor opinion of women.

The cat at No. 3 was a tabby called Martha. Her owner was a long-distance truck driver who was away a great deal. His wife hated cats, and only let Martha live there because she was such a good ratter. Rats came out from the canal banks and terrified the women in Pig Lane. Martha caught a rat nearly every night, so she was allowed to remain.

Beyond No. 3 the houses were on the down-grade. Gone were the shining windows and neat gravel paths of Nos. 1, 2, and 3. No. 4 and No. 5 were joined together and both had shabby brick-work and flaking paint. The gates hung crookedly on their hinges and grass forced its way through the concrete of the front paths.

At No. 4 lived Snowy, the sweetest, gentlest old

cat imaginable. She never had a bad thought or did an unkind action. She couldn't even bring herself to kill rats. She belonged to an old man who lived alone and cooked for himself in a messy, untidy sort of way.

No. 5 was the home of Pete, a black kitten with a white shirt front who led a miserable life. He was constantly being pulled about and teased by a little horror of a boy to whom he had been given for Christmas. Pete was rapidly developing a very bad temper, which was not surprising. He was an extremely unhappy little cat.

House No. 6 was in the last stages of decay, with broken windows mended with cardboard and a door which never quite shut. It belonged to a sailor – who was hardly ever at home – and his wife and daughter. The cat, Sam, was a Manx and had no tail. This was not the result of an accident, it was the way he was born. No true Manx cat has a tail, and they spend all their lives trying to make people believe it, which sours them. No one, least of all a cat, likes jokes made about his appearance.

The seventh house, right down on the canal bank, was really hardly a house at all. It was a shack, and a disgrace to the town. It was occupied by an old man who bought rags and bones. He went around the town with a very old pony and cart, and brought back loads of rubbish to sort over in his backyard. His cat was a huge gray

tom, scarred all over from fighting, with half an ear missing and only one good eye. His name was Pyewacket, and he was the smartest, most

cunning cat in the whole street and the whole town and probably in the whole world.

The seven cats of Pig Lane considered the vacant lot as being especially their own. They couldn't keep the other town cats out, but they could be, and they were, unpleasant to them whenever they met. Even Snowy, who was incapable of being unpleasant to anybody, would turn her back on them and walk away, and her little pink nose got noticeably pinker and the white hairs on her back would begin to rise. Chi Ki, being a Siamese, threw his weight about like anything, and was beastly to the town cats in a maddeningly superior way. Pete, the kitten, was just plain impudent. Martha used language no real lady ought to know, while Sam the Manx and Ginger fought the other toms with the greatest delight. But it was Pyewacket whom the town cats really feared. No one cared to meet Pyewacket on a dark night, for there was something queer about him, they said. He wasn't natural, they said, and they told each other that he had a very strange look in his good eye. No one knew which bold cat had been responsible for biting off half Pyewacket's left ear, but everyone agreed it must have been done a long, long time ago. No cat they knew would dare enter into battle with

16

the great, the terrible, the uncanny Pyewacket.

But to the other six cats of Pig Lane, Pyewacket was both leader and friend. Snowy said *she* always found him to be a perfect gentleman, and Martha agreed. Sam and Ginger admired him tremendously, Pete the kitten hero-worshipped him, and even Chi Ki had been heard to say that old Pye was an awfully decent chap. Which only goes to show that nobody is bad all through.

One thing puzzled the other six cats for a long time, and that was how Pyewacket had come by such an outlandish name. The town was full of cats called Tom or Blackie or Pusskins or Fluff, but – Pyewacket! Whoever heard of such a name? Eventually they did find out, and it was Pye-wacket himself who told them.

All the cats of Pig Lane had met that night near the gorse bushes on the vacant lot. There was a story that a rabbit had been seen there, but it turned out to be nothing but a very old teddy bear, bald with age, which some baby had thrown out of its pram.

It was a warm night in June, and the moon was bright. Everyone felt relaxed and lazy, so that when Ginger suggested a ratting expedition no one was at all keen.

"Can't be bothered," said Martha, and began

washing her paws. They were white paws and she was very proud of them and took a great pride in keeping them nice.

Chi Ki yawned widely, showing the bright pink inside of his mouth and his white, pointed teeth. "Let's just sit and chat," he suggested. "Intelligent conversation is a very civilized way of passing the time."

"Huh?" asked Ginger, looking blank.

"Chi means it's clever to talk," said Pyewacket grinning wickedly. "He should know!"

"Not just *any* sort of talk!" exclaimed Chi Ki impatiently. "Conversation is the er – well – it's – er—"

"Is it asking questions?" asked Pete eagerly. "Things like what happened to Sam's tail?"

"No, it's *not*!" yelled Chi. "Anyway, everyone knows Sam never had a tail. Manx cats are born without them."

"Why?" asked Pete curiously.

"I don't know," confessed Chi. "Sam, do you know?"

"Haven't a clue," said Sam lazily. "I don't mind though; it's one less thing to have to wash."

"Well, really!" said Martha. "You're no gentleman, Sam."

"Never said I was," grunted Sam. "All I know

is that I'm a Manx cat from the Isle of Man, which is somewhere in the sea off the west coast of England, and Manx cats never had tails."

"They did in the past," said Pyewacket, in a deep, mysterious voice. "And I know why they lost them."

"Do you?" asked everyone in chorus, and Snowy added, "I wish you'd tell us. I must confess I've often wondered."

"Once upon a time—" began Pyewacket.

"Oh, good!" said Pete. "It's going to be a fairy tale."

"No it isn't," said Pyewacket, "it's true. And if you interrupt me again I'll send you home."

"Sorry," said Pete. "Go on."

"Once upon a time," Pyewacket began again, "there was a witch. She lived in sixteen hundred and sixty-seven, which is exactly three hundred years ago."

"You're awfully good at numbers," sighed Ginger admiringly.

"I'm awfully good at everything," said Pyewacket. "Well now, this witch had a cat and his name was – guess!"

All the other cats thought hard.

"Kitty?" suggested Martha at last. Pyewacket shook his head scornfully.

19

"It was a *boy* cat," he said. "Try again."

"I've heard witches' cats used to be called Grimalkin," suggested Chi cautiously. He didn't want Pyewacket scorning him too.

"So they were, very often," said Pyewacket kindly. "But this particular cat was more than a cat. Sometimes he turned into a little black imp, and sometimes he was a toad."

"Golly!" exclaimed Pete. "Some cat!"

"He was what people called the witch's 'familiar'," explained Pyewacket. "That means he helped her with her spells. If I tell you that he was my great-great-great-great-great-grandfather will that give you a clue to his name?"

"Pyewacket!" shouted all the other cats, and Pyewacket grinned.

"Right at last," he said. "Well, to continue my story. This old witch and my great-great-ever-so-great-grandfather went over to the Isle of Man for a holiday, and while they were there the cats (who had tails like any other cat in those days) went out of their way to be rude to Granddad. Very rude they were, making personal remarks about him, and about his friend, the witch."

"Disgraceful!" said Martha, glaring at Sam.

"Don't blame me," said Sam. "It was before my time."

"Your great-great-great-great-grandfather was one of them," said Pyewacket. "In fact he was the worst of the lot."

"How do you know?" demanded Sam.

"I just do," said Pyewacket. "I know lots of things the rest of you don't know."

"Go on with the story," begged Pete. "What happened to the rude cats?"

Pyewacket grinned again. "The witch put a spell on them," he said. "Great Granddad Pyewacket helped her, and they made it a good one, I can tell you. That night, when the moon was full – " he paused impressively while the others looked at him, wide-eyed – "all the Manx cats' tails dropped off, and they've never had any tails since."

There was an awe-struck silence. At last Ginger said, "Did the cats mind?"

"Of course they did," said Pyewacket. "They minded like anything. It was a terrible blow to their pride."

"Oh Pyewacket!" yelled Pete. "Can you do spells too?"

"Ah-ha!" said Pyewacket. "That would be telling."

"Well, tell then," begged Chi Ki.

Pyewacket smiled lazily, but made no reply.

21

"I'll bet he can!" said Pete. "I'll bet Pye-wacket can do *anything*. I'll bet he can fly if he wants to. I'll bet his great Granddad used to fly on the witch's broomstick. I'll bet—"

"Shut up," said Chi Ki. "You talk too much for a kitten. If Pyewacket wanted to fly he'd have a spaceship nowadays not a broomstick. Wouldn't you, old chap?"

"Very probably," said Pyewacket carelessly, "only, as it happens, I don't want to fly. I'll tell you what I do want, and I want it very badly. I want to get rid of all the humans in Pig Lane so that we can have it to ourselves."

There was a startled silence. No one was sure if Pyewacket was really serious or if this was one of his jokes. He often made jokes no one quite understood, and he got angry if they didn't laugh.

At last old Snowy said gently: "Get rid of the humans, Pyewacket? But why? If all the people left who would give us our food?"

"My old man never gives me food as it is," said Pyewacket scornfully. "I find it for myself. There's plenty to eat if you know where to look. Humans are a nuisance, there's no two ways about it. Look at poor little Pete, mauled about by that disgusting small boy. Look at Chi, shut in the house all day. Look at Ginger, thrown out on the coldest nights. If we got rid of the people we could do exactly as we pleased all the time. It would be splendid, and I know how to do it!"

"You wouldn't – kill them, would you?" whispered Martha, and a shiver ran down her tabby back.

"Not necessary," said Pyewacket. "No, my friends, we'll frighten them away!"

II *The Promise of Pan*

The six cats looked at Pyewacket with round, astonished eyes. They were so surprised by what he had said that not one of them even noticed a bold rat who ventured out from behind an old tin bathtub and made a rude face at them. The rat went back to his friends and boasted about having had a terrific fight with seven cats and defeating them all, but no one believed him because he was known to be the biggest storyteller on the whole of the canal bank.

Sam was the first to break the silence.

"Er—" he said. "I – er – I don't quite see what you mean, Pye, old friend."

The other cats murmured agreement. How could seven cats frighten a whole street of people out of their homes?

"Easy," said Pyewacket scathingly, grinning round at his circle of friends. The moonlight was reflected in his one good eye so that it shone like a lamp. His torn ear stuck up aggressively and his sharp white teeth gleamed as he grinned. "People are very easy to scare, you know. They're frightened of anything they don't understand. Things are going to happen in Pig Lane that they won't be able to understand at all."

"Such as what?" asked Pete excitedly.

"Oh, bumps and bangs and squeaks all over the house," said Pyewacket, grinning more wickedly than ever. "Dishes bouncing off the table and smashing on the floor. Milk bottles spilled all over the front step. Hoards of mice and rats."

"Dead ones?" asked Ginger. "We'll have to work overtime to account for hoards."

"No," said Pyewacket, "live ones. I'll arrange that. I'll strike a bargain with them. We'll all promise to give up hunting if they'll promise to go and live in the houses. It will be a very good arrangement for them and it'll move the humans quicker than anything else."

"They'll call in the rat catcher," objected Martha.

"Probably they will, and what will he do?" demanded Pyewacket. "I'll tell you. He'll set traps and put down poison. If we keep the rats and mice well-fed they won't be tempted to take the bait. We'll steal from the butchers and give them regular rations on condition that they eat nothing except what they get from us, and steer clear of traps. Rats aren't silly. They know which side their bread's buttered all right."

"But do you think they'll trust us?" asked Snowy doubtfully. "We've always been enemies, so why should they believe us when we say we're going to give them food and leave them alone?"

"That's right," agreed Chi. "On the face of it it doesn't seem likely, now does it?"

Pyewacket looked round the circle and hesitated. At last he said, "Look here, I'm going to tell you something which is known only to a few, a very few, animals. It's a secret, passed down from father to son, and it goes back thousands of years. I know it, but I'm pretty sure none of you do. The chief rat of this town knows it, too. Don't ask me how I know, but I do."

"What is it?" asked Ginger, and he and all the other cats crept a little closer to Pyewacket, who had dropped his voice to a thrilling whisper.

"It's the Promise of Pan," said Pyewacket impressively. "You know who Pan is, don't you?"

"I don't," said Pete.

"Then it's time you did," said Martha severely. "Really, the way some of you kittens are dragged up! Pan is the great spirit who cares for animals. He looks like a human boy, except that he has horns, and the legs and feet of a goat."

"He plays Pan's pipes," put in Snowy. "He lives in the woods and no one ever sees him except animals, and even they don't see him very often. He helps them when they are hurt. But I've never heard of his promise, Pyewacket. What is it?"

"It's a bit difficult to explain," said Pyewacket, scratching behind his torn ear. "It was a kind of arrangement he made thousands of years ago when the animals first began fighting each other. Until then they had all lived at peace, but something happened to start them quarrelling, or perhaps it was just that they got tired of being vegetarians and thought it would be a good idea to eat one another. Anyway, it got worse and worse. Pan tried to stop it but even he couldn't, so he called all the heads of the different animals together and made them agree to his promise, and it's lasted ever since."

"Yes, but what is the promise?" asked Chi Ki impatiently.

"It's a truce," explained Pyewacket. "You promise that for a certain time you won't try and kill the other fellow, and he promises he won't kill you. It's only used in times of emergency. Wild animals cut off by floods use it, for instance. And I can use it to persuade the rats and mice that, for a time at least, they will have nothing to fear from us."

"Sure?" asked Sam doubtfully.

"Of course I'm sure. All I've got to do is see the chief rat – he lives on the canal bank not far from my place – and say, 'Promise of Pan'. He'll listen to me then, and I'll explain our plan."

"You think they'll do it?" asked Ginger, and Pyewacket laughed.

"Why not? They'll have a wonderful time. Free grub, the run of all the houses with not a single cat lifting a paw against them, and lots of fun scaring the people. Oh, they'll love every minute of it."

"I'm not sure I want my poor old man scared," said Snowy.

"Poor old man nothing!" said Pyewacket scornfully. "Who went away last summer to stay with his daughter and left you all on your own? For all he cared you might have starved."

"It's true," said Snowy sadly. "He did."

"I won't worry a bit about my two," said Chi Ki. "They only keep me because they think it's a snob thing to do, to own a Siamese. They don't love me at all."

"I wouldn't want my two old women hurt," said Ginger. "I can do without them and their

28

fussy ways, but I won't have them scared by rats."

"Perhaps a tiny little ghost would make them move out?" suggested Pyewacket. "Just a few moans in the night, eh? Perhaps the merest clanking of chains?"

"Yes, all right," said Ginger. "Only no force."

"You can do anything you like to my family," said Pete. "Especially to the boy."

"Don't be revengeful, dear," said Snowy gently. "Perhaps he doesn't know any better."

"Then it's time he learned," said Pyewacket. "A few rats in the house will do him a world of good."

"But do you really think all this will make them go away?" asked Martha. "Humans tend to cling to their homes. Where would they go?"

"There are other houses," said Pyewacket carelessly. "The town is full of houses. Let them go to some other district. After all, Pig Lane isn't very nice for humans, is it? We'll be doing them a good turn, in making them go. Ten to one they really want to move, only they can't quite make up their minds. All we would be doing is giving them a little, just the gentlest little push."

"Yes, of course," said Martha. "I'm sure you're right, Pyewacket. And when they're all gone we will live here alone?"

"Peacefully," said Pyewacket, looking at each cat in turn with his queer green eye.

"Coming and going whenever we like and no fuss about muddy feet?" said Sam.

"Sleeping in the best beds?" said Ginger. "Squashy quilts all to ourselves!"

"What about milk?" asked Pete. Pyewacket gave a scornful grunt.

"Only kittens need milk," he said. "You want to grow up, Pete."

"But I like milk!" objected Pete.

"Then knock over a milk bottle," said Ginger. "Goodness knows there are enough of them around the town every morning. Why, even the blue tits help themselves to the cream."

"We could give parties," said Chi Ki excitedly. "There are some wonderful chairs with thick, squashy cushions in my people's sitting room. I'm always being chased off them because *she* says I leave hairs, but when the whole house belongs to me I'll invite you all in. We'll sit on the chairs and the sofa, and I'll steal some fish from down the road and we'll crush bones into the hearth rug. Oh boy, this is going to be great!"

"How long do you think it will take to get rid of all the people?" asked Sam.

Pyewacket considered. "Some will be more

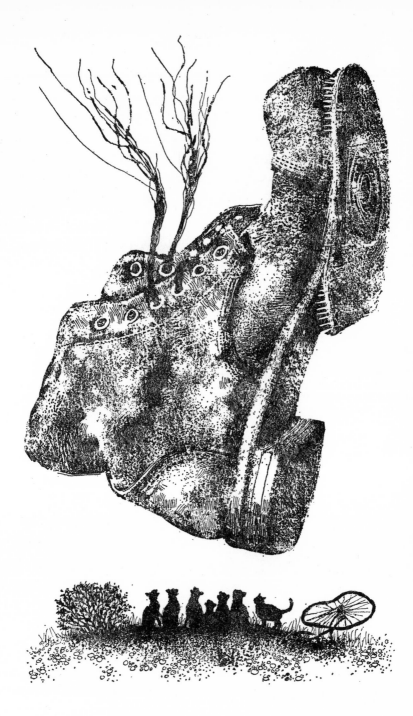

stubborn than others," he said. "My old man, for instance, will be very hard to budge. A few rats mean nothing to him, and I'm sure he doesn't believe in ghosts. Ginger's family, on the other hand, will be easy, and I don't imagine we'll have much trouble with Sam's."

"The old man is always away at sea," agreed Sam. "That only leaves the missus and the girl, and they hate Pig Lane anyway. I often hear them talking about how much they'd like a new house in the suburbs."

"Let's say three months to clear out the whole lot," said Pyewacket. "Now remember, everybody, no weakening. United we stand! Everyone who promises faithfully to do his or her best say miaou!"

Seven voices were raised in an ear-splitting miaou! A window in Pig Lane creaked open and an old boot came sailing over the fence into the vacant lot.

"Scat!" shouted an angry voice.

"I'm off to see the chief rat," whispered Pyewacket, and melted into the shadow of a broken-down Ford car.

III *Mystery in Pig Lane*

The next few days saw a great deal of activity in Pig Lane. The six cats visited one another, constantly talking over the great plan. Pyewacket, as the leader, hurried hither and thither, not saying much to anyone, but obviously full of important thoughts. The most the other cats could get out of him was a sly wink and a murmured, "Hi there", or "See you". He spent a good deal of time down on the canal bank, and it was assumed by the other cats that he was in conference with the chief rat.

The humans seemed unusually active too. On Monday a man in a bowler hat came down the street, knocking at every house and delivering some papers. As soon as he had gone, two workmen arrived with a ladder and put up a large sign. They fastened it to the hoarding on the other side of the road and whatever it said seemed to make everyone very angry.

The cats could not read, but they wished very much that they knew what the sign said. They

c

hung around and listened to the conversations which went on over their heads.

"A scandal!" exclaimed Chi Ki's master, his trim little moustache bristling with indignation. "I never heard of such a thing in my life!"

"Without so much as by your leave or with your leave!" chimed in one of the old ladies who owned Ginger.

"It'll be the end of me," mourned Snowy's old man.

"What can be the matter?" whispered Martha to Sam. "I've never seen humans so upset."

"Search me," said Sam. Then a dreadful thought struck him, and he gasped, "Martha! You don't think that notice says anything about Pyewacket's plan?"

"No, of course not. How could it?" said Martha. "That's a human notice board, that is. It has nothing to do with us cats."

"You never know what Pyewacket is up to," said Sam darkly.

"Pyewacket may be a very clever cat," retorted Martha. "I'm not saying he isn't, but even Pyewacket couldn't write a notice in human language and get two men to hang it on the fence."

"Not unless he really can do spells," said Sam uneasily.

"Oh, rubbish!" said Martha.

That evening all the people in Pig Lane began popping in and out of each other's houses and talking, talking, talking. The only person who didn't join in was Pyewacket's old man, who just went on sorting rags in his backyard. But all the others became friendlier than they had ever been before. The hairdresser and his wife were seen talking to the sailor's wife at No. 6 just as if they were equals. Chi was astonished, because he had often heard them say that those people from No. 4 downward really lowered the tone of the whole street.

That night Pyewacket called a meeting on the vacant lot. Pete, the kitten, went around with a message, saying, "Ten o'clock at the Ford car." Everyone was there on the dot, dying to hear if Pyewacket knew what all the excitement was about. But he didn't know, any more than the rest of them.

"It's queer," he said. "They couldn't have got wind of our plan because nothing has been settled yet. Oh yes, I've seen the chief rat, and I'll tell you about that presently. But that notice board – I can't understand what it can be."

"It can't say anything nice," said Ginger. "They're all very upset."

"Not half as upset as they'll be when we get going," chuckled Pyewacket.

"It's got something to do with the papers that the man wearing the bowler hat delivered," said Martha. "And he came from the town hall. I know him by sight, because I used to visit a cousin of mine who lives with the caretaker there. The papers and the notice are telling them they've got to do something they don't want to do, I'm sure of that."

Pyewacket got to his feet and stretched. Then he yawned, showing his red tongue and his sharp white teeth. "Well, goodnight all," he said.

"You're not going, are you?" exclaimed Ginger. "You haven't told us yet how you got on with the chief rat?"

"Nobody seems interested," said Pyewacket shortly. "All you can talk about is some silly notice board."

He stalked away among the grass and brambles while the other six stared after him in dismay.

"Stop him, someone!" implored Snowy, and Sam dashed after the retreating gray form.

"I say! Don't go! We're awfully sorry!" he gasped. "We're dying to know all about the Promise of Pan."

Pyewacket did not answer, but he stopped and

pretended to examine some old chicken bones which lay in his path.

"*Please*, Pyewacket," said Sam.

"Oh, very well then," said Pyewacket, and he walked back to the group, rather stiff-legged.

"Well?" asked everyone eagerly.

"Well what?" said Pyewacket, and he licked his front foot carefully, removing a speck of mud.

"Well, what did he say?" asked Pete.

"What was the outcome of your interview with our erstwhile enemy the rat?" said Chi Ki, casting a withering look upon the kitten. Chi Ki believed in keeping youngsters in their place, and it was not Pete's place to put questions to the great Pyewacket.

"Oh, him," said Pyewacket grandly. "I didn't have any trouble with him. All he's anxious about is that all of you thoroughly understand the Promise of Pan. If he and the other rats come forward to help us, he doesn't want any – er – unfortunate mistakes. There is to be a truce until all the humans have been driven from Pig Lane. After that, we go back to our old ways and it's every animal for himself. That goes for the mice as well," he added as an afterthought.

"Not kill one tiny, weeny little mouse?" asked Pete wistfully.

"Not one," Pyewacket told him sternly. "If you must hunt, hunt beetles, but leave the mice alone."

"Do we have to swear a tremendous oath?" asked Sam eagerly, but old Snowy said, "No, don't let's have any swearing, please. I'm quite sure if we all promise, it will do just as well."

"Promise then," said Pyewacket. "Say after me, 'I promise that until the last human is driven from Pig Lane I will look upon the mice and rats as my friends and allies and I will not hunt or kill them under any circumstances whatever.' "

There was a general murmur as the six cats repeated the solemn promise.

"Hope it won't take too long," said Ginger, "I will miss my daily mouse."

"Me too," said Sam. "We're paying a high price for Pig Lane, Pyewacket. Suppose it takes three months to get the humans to go. That's ninety mice I shan't have eaten. A fortune!"

"But worth it," Pyewacket assured him. "Just think of having the whole street to ourselves. And then there'll be the glory of it. We'll probably be the only cats in the whole world to take over a street from humans. We'll be in the history books. The Battle of Pig Lane, 1967!"

"Under the inspired leadership of General Pyewacket," said Chi.

"Three cheers for General Pyewacket!" Pete yelled. "Hip, hip—"

"Pipe down," said Pyewacket severely. "Do you want the whole town to hear you? Listen to me, all of you. We have a tough job ahead, a very tough job. I don't say we can't do it, but—" He paused and looked around the circle of faces – "you're not exactly a first rate army, are you? One kitten, two ladies, a foreigner—"

"Meaning me?" asked Sam dangerously. "I'll have you know the Isle of Man is as British as—"

"Not meaning you," said Pyewacket. "Meaning Chi Ki. Oh, he's a very good chap and I'm sure he'll give an excellent account of himself in battle, but—"

Chi Ki rose, stretched lazily and stalked over to where Pyewacket was standing. His tail was straight up in the air, stiff as a ramrod, and his bright blue eyes looked dangerous.

"You want to make something out of it, Pyewacket?" he asked. He twisted his head sideways, like a puma, and hissed.

"Oh please don't!" cried Snowy nervously. "Please, boys, no fighting among ourselves!"

Pyewacket's green eye stared straight into Chi's blue ones. His tail began to lash. Everyone held his breath.

39

Then suddenly Pyewacket laughed. "Calm down, old chap," he said. "Can't you take a joke?"

"Yes, if it was a joke," said Chi Ki.

"Of course it was a joke," said Martha. "No one really looks upon you as a foreigner, Chi dear. You're one of *us*."

"All right then," said Chi Ki, still a little stiffly, and he turned and went back to his place.

"Sam and Ginger are good fighters," said Pyewacket. "So that makes four of us, with Chi. Four of us against a whole street of people."

"We've got the rats on our side," Ginger reminded him.

"And the mice," said Martha. "Mice may be small but they're very important. Elephants are terrified of them, so I've heard."

Pyewacket snorted. "There are no elephants in Pig Lane," he reminded her shortly.

"Well, there's no need to be sarcastic!" retorted Martha with spirit. "If they can frighten elephants they can frighten people, or so one would suppose. Correct me, Pyewacket, if I'm wrong."

"They frighten women," said Pyewacket, grinning at her wickedly. "But then females scare easily."

"They don't!" cried Martha and Snowy with one voice.

"Now look here," said Sam. "We've had enough arguments for one evening. If we're going to carry this plan through we've got to pull together. It doesn't matter if you're a male, a female or a kitten like Pete here, there'll be jobs for all of us. We won't only need strong fighters, we'll need quick thinkers, and quick movers. Martha and Snowy will have their part to play and so will little Pete. So where do we go from here? Pyewacket, we take our orders from you."

"All of you be here this time tomorrow and I'll have your orders ready for you," said Pyewacket. "In the meantime, watch your humans, and note their weak spots. It's on their fears and their weakness that we've got to make war!"

"I can't help feeling sorry for them," said old Snowy sadly.

"No need to be sorry," Pyewacket told her. "No harm will come to them. We're only going to drive them away."

IV *Pyewacket gives his Orders*

The following day passed slowly for the six cats under Pyewacket's command. They were waiting nervously for the meeting that night and wondering just what they would be required to do.

For some reason all the humans in Pig Lane seemed nervous too. It was easy to see that they had something on their minds, and whatever it was made them impatient and cross. Chi Ki was thankful when his two had finished their breakfast and hurried off to the shop. He knew they must be very upset about something because they even forgot to shut him in the kitchen as they usually did. As soon as they were safely out of the way, he strolled into the sitting room and curled up in one of the big, comfortable armchairs.

"This is the life," said Chi Ki to himself. "A chap needs his comforts. I will spend a lot of time in this chair when I've got the place to myself."

Poor little Pete was less fortunate. The small boy who owned him was at home from school with a bad head cold and he spent the day snuffling and sneezing, and squeezing Pete round the middle to make him squeal. At last, Pete couldn't stand it any longer and he put out his claws and scratched. Then the small boy squealed too, and his mother came running, and slapped them both. Pete retreated under the kitchen sink and crouched there buzzing angrily.

"If this goes on much longer I'll remain bad-tempered for life," he thought. "Oh, I *do* hope Pyewacket's great plan succeeds!"

At No. 2, the house with the very clean muslin curtains, Ginger was in trouble also. His two old ladies seemed to have made up their minds to have a grand cleaning of every drawer and cupboard in the house, and there was no peace to be found anywhere. They shooed Ginger from the kitchen to the sitting room, and out of there into the hall, and finally upstairs, where it was peaceful until after lunch, and then they started on the wardrobes in the bedrooms.

"We shall have to get rid of almost everything," he heard one of them say, and the other said mournfully, "It's not going to be the same thing at all, Sarah. Four flights up, and my poor old legs!" Ginger had no idea what she was talking about.

Snowy's old man seemed to spend the day deep

in thought. He never did much in the way of housework or cooking, and today he did nothing at all. He just sat in his shabby old armchair puffing at his pipe and thinking. The room grew so full of smoke that Snowy nearly choked. He forgot to give her any dinner, and altogether she had a miserable day.

Martha was luckier. She escaped from the house first thing in the morning when the door was opened so that the milk could be taken in. The truck driver was away as usual, but his wife and daughter had been talking excitedly from the moment they woke up. They sat in the kitchen with their hair in curlers, drinking cups of strong tea and talking away like mad. Martha thought they seemed pleased about something, because every now and then one of them would say, "So now he'll have to do something about it, and it's a good thing too!"

Martha slipped past the daughter as she stooped to pick up the bottle of milk and wandered off down Pig Lane. She hoped to see Pyewacket, but there was no sign of him at the shack where he lived. She said good morning to the pony as he was led out of the yard drawing the shabby little cart, and he nodded back at her in his usual dejected way. The rag-and-bone man was muttering angrily to himself, and seemed madder than ever.

Soon, Sam turned up. Martha saw him wandering along the side of the lane by the tall fence looking very much at a loose end.

"Hello, Sam," she said. "All the humans seem very odd today. You don't think they could have possibly got wind of the plan, do you?"

"Don't see how," said Sam, sitting down in a patch of sunlight. "After all, nothing has happened yet, and it isn't as if any of us could give away the secret because none of the humans can speak cat language. But they do seem queer, Martha, you're right there. My old woman is busy writing a letter to Master, who's away at sea. I heard her say so to young Beverley before she went off to school. She was upset about something, but I couldn't make out what it was."

"It all began with the man from the town hall," said Martha. "I wish I could read. I can understand a good bit of what humans say, but I've never met a cat yet who could read what they write."

"Pyewacket probably can if he wants to," said Sam.

Martha shook her head.

"I doubt it," she said. "If he could, he'd tell us

45

what is on that notice. That's got something to do with the mystery, too."

"Oh well, it has nothing to do with us," said Sam, but there he was quite wrong.

By ten o'clock that night it was raining, a steady, drenching rain which sent the cats scurrying to the shelter of the old Ford car. They held their meeting huddled on the back seat, trying to avoid the drips which came through the holes in the roof. Everyone was feeling tense and anxious, except for Pyewacket. He came late, after everyone else had arrived, and appeared to be in the best of spirits.

"Evening all," he said jauntily, entering gracefully through a broken window. "Well, it's been a busy day."

"It may have been for you," grumbled Chi Ki, "I've been bored to tears. My people came home nearly two hours late this evening. Goodness knows where they went after they closed the shop, but they seemed to be more cheerful. *He* said something about things turning out for the best and *she* laughed and said, 'It's an ill wind—' "

"I'm glad somebody is happy," said Ginger. "My two old girls have been crying on and off all day. The man in the bowler hat came to call this

afternoon, but even that didn't cheer them up."

"Why should it?" asked Martha.

"You'd think they'd like a gentleman visitor," said Ginger.

Martha snorted. "What conceit!" she exclaimed. "Just because he's a man—"

"Shut up," said Pyewacket rudely. "You aren't here to talk about men in bowler hats. You're here to get your battle orders from me."

"Fire away," said Sam. He ducked to try and avoid a splash of rain, then licked his damp coat impatiently. "How I hate being wet!" he exclaimed.

"I'm hungry," whined Pete. "No one gave me my supper. They've all gone out to the movies and never even gave me a thought. Can I go and catch a mouse, Pyewacket?"

" *No!*" shouted Pyewacket sternly. "That's the first order I have to give you. No more hunting. The Promise of Pan starts tonight."

"Poor little Pete," said Snowy gently. "I cannot bear to think of a kitten going hungry."

Pyewacket gave an impatient shake and drops of rain flew off his fur in all directions.

"Some army I've got," he remarked bitterly. "Hungry kittens and soft old grandmothers."

Ginger and Chi Ki exchanged glances. Really,

48

Pyewacket's manners left much to be desired.

"Steady, old boy," said Chi.

Pyewacket ignored him. "I will now give all of you your orders," he announced. "Chi – you have the loudest voice of all of us. Your job is to use it. Screech all night. Keep people awake. Let yourself go!"

"It will be a pleasure," said Chi. "I know one or two Siamese battle songs—"

"They'll do fine," said Pyewacket. "But watch yourself, mate. They'll throw things at you."

"I will be on the alert," Chi promised solemnly.

"Next, Ginger. Get up into the attic, Ginger, and stamp about over your old ladies' bedroom ceiling. You can give a few weird cries too, if you like. Remember, you're a ghost."

"A fat, yellow ghost!" said Pete, and giggled. Ginger shot him an angry look.

"Hush, dear," said Snowy. "Don't be silly. Ginger is marmalade, not yellow, and he is a fine figure of a cat. Those bulges are muscle, not fat."

"Martha!" said Pyewacket sharply. "Pay attention please. Your job is to steal. Steal everything you can get hold of and leave it out for the rats. I've arranged for a positive army of rats to invade your place, and they must be fed. Leave the food on the sitting-room floor and then keep out of the way. Some of them are a bit nervous in spite of the Promise of Pan, and your reputation as a rat catcher is known all over the town."

"I'll keep out of the way all right," promised Martha. "If I saw them, I'd never be able to control my teeth and claws."

"Sam, you'll break things," said Pyewacket. "Walk along the dresser shelves and knock off the china. Chuck down the ornaments. Tear open the cushions and let the feathers out. Do all the damage you can."

"My word, that's going to hit them where it hurts," said Sam. "My old woman is very bad-tempered. She'd kill me if I get caught."

"Then don't get caught," advised Pyewacket. "Remember, this is war. Pete!"

The kitten jumped guiltily. He had been in a dream, thinking wistfully about food. "Yes, Pyewacket?" he said.

"I'll want you with me, to act as a messenger. You're too small to do much on your own, but you can be very useful taking messages to the mice and rats."

"O.K., chief," said Pete joyfully. "Will do!"

"You've forgotten Snowy," Martha said.

Pyewacket looked thoughtfully at the white cat's kind old face.

"No, I haven't forgotten Snowy," he said.

"I don't think I could bring myself to do anything violent, my dear," said Snowy anxiously.

"And I won't ask you to," Pyewacket assured her. "All I ask you to do is – nothing. If the mice and rats arrive just leave them alone. They won't harm your old man. They may keep him awake, they may eat his food and chew his belongings, but they won't touch him."

"I'm glad," said Snowy with relief. "I'm on your side in this plan, Pyewacket, and I always stand by my friends, but I've lived with my old man for a long time now and I wouldn't have him hurt for the world."

"What are you going to do, Pyewacket?" asked Sam curiously.

"Oh, this and that," said Pyewacket lightly. "I'll sing a duet with Chi and break a little crockery with Sam. I might even join Ginger up in his attic. I'll be around."

"And I'll be with you!" exclaimed Pete excitedly. "My word, Pyewacket, we'll soon drive out the humans at this rate, won't we?"

Pyewacket smiled lazily. His green eye glittered and his paws moved softly up and down, up and down, on the old leather seat of the car.

"I think we will, my friends," he said grimly. "Yes, indeed, I really think we will!"

V *The Monsters Move In*

Next day the rats advanced upon Pig Lane. They came up stealthily from the banks of the canal before it was light, moving like shadows. They slipped silently through half-open windows or chewed through the old, rotten woodwork of the doors. Soon, every house in Pig Lane was invaded by scuttling feet and gnawing teeth. Bright, beady eyes peeped out of holes in the walls, long whiskers twitched, long tails were glimpsed flicking around the corners.

"Where are the mice?" demanded Pyewacket, meeting the chief rat by appointment in the coal shed of No. 5. "They should be here by now."

The chief rat grinned.

"You'll have to count them out," he said. "They won't come. They say we can manage very well without them and they don't really believe in the Promise of Pan. You can't blame them, Pyewacket. They're small, you know, and easily caught. I suppose you fellows must catch at least twenty mice for every single rat?"

"That's not the point," said Pyewacket sternly. "Orders are orders."

"Tell that to the mice," retorted the chief rat. "Anyway, what do we want them for? We're doing very nicely without them."

"How are you getting on?" asked Pete eagerly. In his job as messenger boy he was lurking at Pyewacket's heels.

"Nicely, thank you, little feller," said the chief rat condescendingly. Pyewacket glanced at him sharply.

"Don't get ideas," he said warningly. "We may be working together just at present under the Promise of Pan but that doesn't alter the fact that we're cats and you're only a rat. Say 'sir' when you speak to Pete. He may be a kitten now, but he'll be a big cat some day."

"Call me sir! Call me sir!" yelled Pete in high excitement.

"Oh very well – *sir*!" said the chief rat in a rage. "And what would your majesty like us to do next?"

"Just carry on," said Pyewacket grandly, and he strolled out of the coal shed in a lordly manner, Pete running close behind.

The chief rat, pale with rage, went back into No. 5 and nearly frightened the life out of Pete's small boy by climbing to the top of the wardrobe and then landing with a plop on the floor by the bed.

"Mummy, mummy!" yelled the boy. "Come quick! There's a huge rat in my room and it's going to bite me!"

"Oh my goodness gracious me!" exclaimed his mother. "Rats in the house! Where's that useless kitten of yours? It's time we were out of this old place and no mistake."

With trembling fingers she threw a hairbrush at the chief rat. He grinned, and disappeared down a hole in the floor.

And so it went on all through that day and the next day and the next. Every night the seven cats met by the old car and compared notes, and every night each one had some story to tell of the awful discomforts the humans were having to endure, and how restless and dissatisfied they were becoming.

On the fourteenth night Chi Ki was able to report a big step forward in their scheme.

"My people are going to move!" he announced breathlessly as soon as he joined the group. "It's true, they really are! They've found an apartment in a new block the other side of the town and they're moving at the end of the month!"

"Well done, Chi!" said Pyewacket. "You must have worked really hard."

"It was more the rats, I think," said Chi Ki modestly. "They've given them no peace. *She* found a small rat sitting in the sugar bowl this morning. Oh dear, it was funny! I thought I'd die laughing!"

"You'll have to watch out that they don't take you with them," warned Ginger. "You'd have a long walk back from the other side of the town."

"Besides," said Snowy, "they might butter your paws and shut you in until you are settled."

"I wouldn't settle!" Chi Ki told her positively. Snowy shook her head.

"You might," she said, "butter on the paws is a powerful charm."

"Well anyway," Chi Ki told her triumphantly, "they won't take me. Cats aren't allowed in the new block. No pets, that's the rule."

"Then what are they planning for you?" demanded Pyewacket, and Chi Ki looked thoughtful.

"I don't know," he said. "They probably think they can give me away."

"You'll have to be on your guard," Pyewacket warned. "At the first sign of a cat basket you must run for it. Come around to my place. You can hide there until they've gone. What about the rest of you? Anything to report?"

"My two old ladies have something up their sleeves," said Ginger. "They're still clearing out drawers, and yesterday they sent a whole lot of stuff to a rummage sale. Why should they do that unless they are going to move?"

"Straws show which way the wind blows," agreed Sam. "My master came back from one of his trips yesterday and his wife told him he must do something about the rats or she'd go crazy. So he set a trap, but, of course, none of the rats will go near it. I keep them much too well fed to be tempted by a stale old bit of cheese. I stole a very nice steak which was meant for Master's supper. The rats relished that, I can tell you. I had a bit myself, and very good it was. The master missed a treat there, and wasn't he wild!"

"We had the Welfare Lady at our place yesterday," said Snowy. "She was very shocked at the state of the house and I heard her tell my old man he'd be better off in the old people's home. I agree with her. He really doesn't look after himself properly, and the rats are the last straw. I believe he'll leave soon."

"Good for you, Snowy!" said Sam.

"Oh, it has nothing to do with me, dear," said

Snowy. "All I want is the best for my poor old man."

"Well, off with all of you," said Pyewacket briskly. "Press on with the good work. Something tells me it won't be long now before we have Pig Lane all to ourselves."

Three days later, at ten o'clock in the morning, Pete was keeping watch for Pyewacket while he went off on some mysterious business of his own. He saw a large green furniture removal van turn the corner into Pig Lane and trundle slowly along looking at the numbers on the doors. As it stopped outside No. 3, the front door was opened by the truck driver's wife, and Martha slipped past her and came flying down the path.

"Drat the cat!" said the woman crossly. "I meant to shut her up before we began moving. Now ten to one she won't be around when we're ready to leave."

"You bet I won't!" giggled Martha in Pete's ear. "Come on, let's clear out of here fast!"

"What's happening?" demanded Pete breathlessly, as he followed her across the lane and through a hole in the fence. Martha did not pause to reply until they reached the sanctuary of the old Ford car.

She jumped through the broken window on to

the back seat, gave herself a few brisk licks while waiting for Pete to follow her, and then said, "They're off, my lot. They've got a house out in the suburbs. Seems they've been waiting for it for ages, although I never knew. When the rats arrived, Master went round to the town hall and made a fuss. Said this old place wasn't fit to live in and the authorities would have to find them a house at once, so they did."

"How do you know all this?" marvelled Pete.

"I keep my eyes and ears open," Martha told him. "I don't pretend to understand every word they say, but I can put two and two together as well as anyone. And I'll tell you something else, Pete. I don't believe your people will be here much longer either."

"Why not?" asked Pete excitedly.

"Just something I picked up," said Martha. "I believe they've been given a house too. My old woman was talking about it. So look out, Pete. Any moment now the furniture van may stop at your door, and you'll be popped into a basket."

"Not me!" said Pete. "If anyone tries to put me in a basket I'll scratch and I'll bite and I'll—"

"Don't boast," said Martha. "Just watch out, that's all. Keep out of the way as I'm doing." She stopped talking and listened intently.

"Do you hear anything?" she asked.

"Someone's calling," whispered Pete.

"Puss – puss – puss!" came a voice from the other side of the fence. "Come along, puss. Kitty, kitty, kitty!"

Martha crouched low on the seat of the car, her ears flattened back against her head.

"They can call till they're blue in the face," she muttered. "They've seen the last of me."

The voice called some more and then said loudly, "Drat the cat! I can't spend any more time looking for her now. I haven't finished packing the china yet. The van came earlier than I'd expected."

"She'll turn up before long," came the voice of the woman who owned Pete. "I'll keep a lookout for her if she doesn't come back before you leave, and we'll bring her along with Pete on Thursday."

"Thursday?" whispered Pete. "Is Thursday soon, Martha? Does she mean they're moving on Thursday, or what?"

"Thursday comes after Wednesday," said Martha, which didn't help Pete at all because he had no idea when Wednesday came. He was just going to ask her about it again when Pyewacket appeared at the window, spotted them, and leaped into the car.

61

"So things are starting to move!" he observed. "It's happening quicker than I thought. Chi's people are off shortly, yours, Martha, are going today, Pete's go on Thursday and Snowy's old man won't be long. Ginger's ladies are packing, so that only leaves Sam and me. I don't know much about the situation in Sam's house but I do know that it'll take a bulldozer to shift my old man."

Pete cocked his ears. "Listen!" he said. "What's that?"

The three cats listened. From the other side of the vacant lot came the sound of a heavy engine and the rattle and thump of machinery. The ground shook, making the old car sway. The sound came nearer and nearer, it roared in their ears. Very cautiously, Pyewacket raised his head and peeped out of the back window. Then his green eyes grew wide and he drew in his breath with a hiss of surprise.

"What is it – oh, what is it?" whispered Martha.

Pyewacket looked at her solemnly. "It's a bulldozer!" he said.

VI *And the Humans Move Out*

For a moment all three cats were too surprised to speak. They stood in a row with their noses pressed to the back window of the old car watching the bulldozer as it advanced on them across the vacant lot.

"Do – do you think it's on its way to get Pyewacket's old man?" Pete whispered fearfully in Martha's ear. "Oh Martha, do you think Pyewacket has cast a spell and *made up* that bulldozer?"

"No, of course not," snapped Martha. She sounded cross because she was rather scared. "I've told you time and time again, Pete, that Pyewacket doesn't do spells. He's just an ordinary cat like you and me."

"He's not!" said Pete indignantly. "Perhaps he doesn't do spells, but he's not an ordinary cat. He's a super duper cat. He's a hero!" He was so excited that he forgot to whisper and fairly shouted the last bit of his speech.

Pyewacket turned his head. "Who's a hero?" he asked.

"You are," said Pete, and then he was so overcome with shyness that he jumped onto the floor and hid under the seat.

"That kitten thinks the world of you," remarked Martha. "Did you hear what he was saying, Pyewacket? He actually thinks that bulldozer is one of your spells! I've told him you can't cast spells—"

"How do you know I can't?" asked Pyewacket sharply.

"Well – nobody can nowadays. It's all nonsense; everybody knows that," said Martha.

Pyewacket gave her a queer look out of his green eye. "I could turn you into a frog," he said. "A frog called Pigwiggin. How would you like that?"

"Oh, get along with you, do!" exclaimed Martha. "You and your old frogs! But joking apart, what do you suppose that bulldozer is doing here?"

"Obviously it's clearing the ground," said Pyewacket. "Perhaps they're going to start building the factory at last."

"Oh dear!" said Martha. "Now that *is* a nuisance. Just as it seemed we were going to have Pig Lane all to ourselves they start to build a horrid great factory all over our playground. There'll be noise and people and cars and smoke and smells—"

"Look!" exclaimed Pyewacket. "Here comes something else!"

Another great mechanical monster had arrived on the vacant lot. This one had two huge arms with pincers on the ends of them, and it was picking up the rubbish and dumping it in the truck at the back. As they watched, it grabbed a broken-down car which lay at some distance from their own and lifted it high in the air. The arms swung, and the car dropped with a clatter and a crash on top of the other litter in the truck. The monster moved on purposefully toward the old Ford.

"Quick!" yelled Pyewacket, and in the wink of an eye the three cats leaped through the broken window and took to their heels. When they reached the fence they paused and looked back. The old Ford car had gone, and the great monster was plunging on toward a heap of iron beds and bicycles. Behind it came the bulldozer, scooping up bushes and earth, levelling everything down. Already the vacant lot was almost unrecognizable. It had ceased to be an exciting playground, and had become just one more building site.

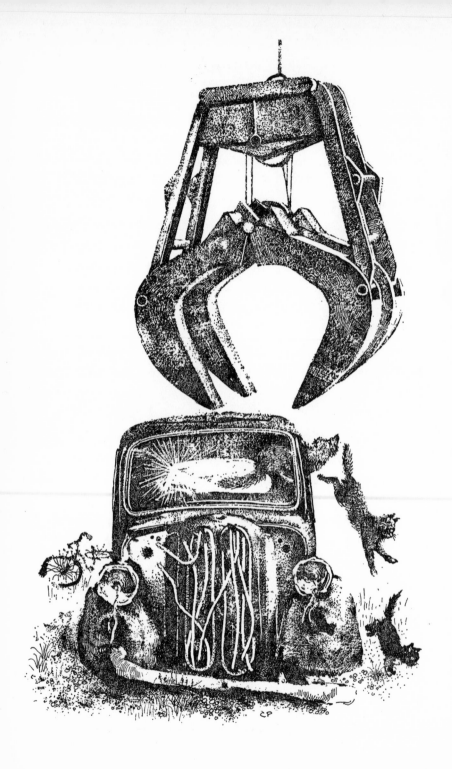

"The march of progress," observed Pyewacket. The other two looked at him respectfully. They had no idea what he meant, but it sounded very grand.

"Ah well," he went on, "we still have Pig Lane and no one is going to change that."

Which just shows that even the cleverest cat can sometimes be wrong.

Martha stayed away, carefully hidden, until the green furniture van drove off from No. 3, with the truck driver's wife perched up in the cab holding her canary in its cage. A few bits of newspaper and straw blew fitfully about the small front garden, and the old gate swung to and fro, squeaking as it swung.

Pete's small boy, who had been watching the removal, picked up a stone and threw it through the front window. The glass tinkled on to the floor inside the empty house and the boy, frightened at what he had done, took to his heels and ran home.

"Thanks very much," said Martha, and jumped gracefully through the broken window.

It felt wonderful to have the whole house to herself. She went proudly through to the kitchen, had a little drink from the dripping tap in the sink, nibbled at the remains of a sandwich left by one of the men and spoke sharply to a rat who was lurking in the larder, telling him he would no longer be required. Then she ran upstairs to the front bedroom window, from which she had an excellent view of everything that went on in Pig Lane.

It was then about six o'clock and a fine, sunny evening. Next door at No. 2, Ginger's old ladies were working in their small garden. They were digging up plants and packing them carefully, with plenty of soil around the roots, into a wooden box. At No. 4, Snowy lay on the doorstep in the sun. The Welfare Lady had to step over her when she arrived, as she presently did. When she came out again, she was followed by the old man who pointed at Snowy and said something which Martha could not hear. The Welfare Lady shook her head decidedly, and the old man looked sad.

A clip-clop of hoofs attracted Martha's attention from the little scene at No. 4. Around the corner from the Market Square came the rag-and-bone man with his pony and cart. The cart was piled high with old iron and bundles of rags and the pony looked tired and depressed. Martha remembered Pyewacket's remark that it would take a bulldozer to shift his old man, and she trembled. The bulldozer was here, so what would happen next? Pig Lane seemed full of danger on this lovely evening in June.

Two days later Pete's family moved out. Pete, who should have been on the alert, had the narrowest of escapes. The small boy captured him and put him into a basket, but before he could fasten the lid Pete got one paw out and scratched the boy severely. The boy dropped the basket with a yell, and Pete jumped out and ran for his life. He made straight for Pyewacket's place, where he found Martha already in hiding.

"Hello, Pete," she said. "I've been expecting you ever since the van arrived. I've kept out of the way because, if you remember, your family said they'd take me along when they left."

"Oh, I've had such an awful adventure!" gasped Pete. "There was a basket, and he put me in and I thought I was done for, only I got one paw out and I scratched—"

"You've only yourself to blame," said Martha sternly. "What were you hanging around for in the first place? You should have cleared out as soon as the van arrived."

"I couldn't. They shut me in the bathroom," said Pete resentfully.

"Oh well, you're safe now, and that's all that matters," said Martha. "I've got a message for you from Pyewacket. He says you're to stay here and lie low until he comes back."

"But it's so dull," grumbled Pete. "As soon as my people leave I want to go and take over the house."

"Oh yes, I daresay," retorted Martha. "And have them come back later to pick you up!"

"I never thought of that," confessed Pete. "But Pyewacket will let me have my house, won't he?"

"I believe he's planning to move in with you," said Martha. "The pony told him this morning that he's heard a tale that the old man is going to be evacuated. That means people will be coming to turn him out of here, and Pyewacket doesn't want to be around when it happens."

"I'll be proud to have him in my house," said Pete. "But why are they turning the old man out?"

"Don't ask me," said Martha. She licked a paw and washed behind her ear. "It's going to rain," she observed, and washed behind the other ear. "Humans do the queerest things. Perhaps Pyewacket's spells *are* making the people move."

"But you said you didn't believe in spells," protested Pete.

"What I say and what I think aren't always the

same," said Martha, and dozed off with her front paws tucked neatly under her chest. Pete was bored. There was no one to talk to and nothing to do.

He wondered how the removal was getting on. Surely there would be no harm in just taking a look? He would be very careful. He glanced at Martha. She was sound asleep. A rat poked its nose out of a hole in a bundle of rags, made a hideous face at Pete and popped in again.

Pete got up cautiously and crossed the yard on silent paws. His own house was only two doors away. If he peeped around the corner of Pyewacket's yard he would be able to see what was going on. Perhaps by now the removal men had finished loading the furniture and had gone, in which case he was going to take possession of No. 5, no matter what Martha might say. He ventured out into the lane.

The removal van was still there, but nothing seemed to be happening. "Where is everybody?" thought Pete curiously, and crept a little nearer. There was no one in the van, and no one in the lane, but as he approached the house he heard the sound of angry voices within.

"Your side!" shouted a man's voice, and another one retorted, "Don't talk so silly! I'm jammed up against the wall as it is. Ease it over your way."

"Take care!" said the small boy's mother. "You'll break it!"

"It's jammed," said the first man, and he sounded angry. "Turn it over sideways, mate."

"It must be the piano," giggled Pete to himself. "It's wedged in the passage. What a joke!"

All three voices were now talking at once, and from the bumps and bangs it sounded as if the piano was taking some knocks. Pete was so amused that he forgot to be cautious, and advanced quite openly into the garden to get a better view.

The next moment he felt himself seized by the scruff of the neck and the small boy's hated voice said triumphantly, "Got you!"

Despair filled Pete's heart, but then out of the blue came deliverance.

With an unearthly screech, Pyewacket himself leaped from the gatepost straight on to the shoulders of the small boy. He yelled even louder than Pyewacket, and bolted for the house. He reached the front door just as one of the removal men came out backwards with his end of the piano. The man staggered and fell over the boy, and the piano, missing them both by inches, shot

down two steps into the garden and fell with a hideous jangle of strings. Everybody shouted at once, and Pyewacket, with Pete giggling at his heels, dashed back to the shelter of the rag-and-bone man's yard.

VII *Accident*

Now that the old Ford car had gone and the mechanical monsters were still hard at work on the vacant lot, the cats had to find a new meeting place. The rag-and-bone man's yard seemed to be the safest and most convenient place. Here, a few days after Pete's family had moved, Chi Ki met Snowy at eleven o'clock on a fine, sunny morning. Snowy looked depressed and Chi was obviously in a highly nervous state.

Pyewacket, who had just returned from one of his mysterious excursions, looked at them both searchingly and said, "What's up with you two? Snowy looks as miserable as Monday morning and Chi's got the jumps."

"My poor old man has gone," said Snowy sadly. "The Welfare Lady came this morning in a car and took him to an old people's home."

"Best place for him," said Pyewacket kindly. "Be sensible, Snowy, you know he couldn't look after himself properly, let alone you."

"I know," said Snowy. "But I miss him just the

same. Besides, I feel guilty. I feel it was the rats that finally drove him out."

"Oh fiddle!" said Pyewacket. "You worry too much, Snowy. And what arrangements did he make for you?"

"He wanted to take me with him but he couldn't," said Snowy. "They don't allow pets in the old people's home. The Welfare Lady said she'd send the Animal Protection Society to catch me, but I didn't wait for them."

"Good job too," said Pyewacket. "You'll be all right on your own."

"I suppose so," said Snowy a little doubtfully. She turned to the Siamese. "And what about you, Chi?"

"I've had a *terrible* experience!" burst out Chi Ki. He was shaking all over and seemed completely unnerved. "*They* sold me to the pet shop! Sold me! Can you imagine? The pet shop man came yesterday and took me away in a basket. I yelled for help, but none of you came."

"Didn't hear you, old chap," said Pyewacket. "Awfully sorry. But you managed to get away?"

"Yes, this morning when the lad was cleaning out the cages," said Chi Ki tremulously. "I clawed him and ran for it, but they'll be after me. They paid quite a lot of money for me, so they'll be sure

76

to want me back. Me in a shop! For sale, like a pound of tomatoes! I've never been so humiliated in my life!"

"Oh, poor Chi!" said Snowy. "When do your people move?"

"Today, I believe," said Chi Ki. "All my dreams of having the house to myself are shattered. I'll never dare to go back even after they leave because that would be the first place the pet shop people would search. And I was looking forward so much to having all those lovely, squashy armchairs to myself."

Pyewacket gave a sarcastic smile. "It never occurred to you, I suppose, that when people move they take their chairs with them?" he said. Chi stared at him speechlessly.

At last he said, "No, it never did. I *am* a Silly Billy. Oh well, without the squashy chairs I don't want the house. I'll stay here with you, Pyewacket, if I may."

"The more the merrier," said Pyewacket. "Martha's here already, so are Pete and Snowy, and now you, so that only leaves Ginger and Sam. I don't think it will be long before Ginger's people move. They've dug up all their plants."

There was a patter of hurrying feet in the yard

77

and Sam appeared, breathless, in the doorway of the shed.

"Come and see what's happening outside!" he said.

The four cats ventured out cautiously into Pig Lane, where they were joined by Martha and Pete.

"Look what they're doing!" gasped Pete. "Pyewacket, look what they're doing! Snowy, look what—"

"Shut up," said Pyewacket.

"But Pyewacket," protested Pete. "They're taking away our fence!"

Down at the far end of Pig Lane two men were working on the high wooden fence, taking down the boards and loading them on to a truck. It made the lane look quite different, and as the bright sunshine shone on the row of old houses they looked older and shabbier and even more derelict than they did before. The green removal van was now standing outside No. 2, and Ginger's old ladies were running backward and forward carrying small objects and getting in the way of the removal men. Ginger himself was nowhere to be seen.

"Puss – puss – puss!" called one of the old ladies.

"Kitty – kitty – kitty!" called the other.

78

"Where do you suppose he is?" Martha whispered, and Pyewacket chuckled.

"He cleared out first thing this morning," he answered. "He's up in the loft over the pony's stable."

"You never told us that!" said Pete.

"Them as don't know can't tell," said Pyewacket briefly. "He'll stay up there until his old ladies have gone."

"Isn't it wonderful the way we're getting rid of them all!" exclaimed Pete. "We are clever, aren't we, Pyewacket? You're the cleverest of course, but we're clever too, aren't we? Martha, we're clever, aren't we? Snowy, we're clever—"

"Very clever, dear," said Snowy. "Of course, the rats have been a great help."

"The Promise of Pan ends today," Pyewacket reminded them. "The chief rat came over to see me about it yesterday. He had an idea we might keep it going for ever – said they found it nice and peaceful not having to be constantly on their guard against us, but I said nothing doing."

"I should think not!" said Sam. "The next thing we know they'd think they were the bosses of Pig Lane. Give a rat an inch and he'll take a mile."

"Puss – puss – puss!" called one of Ginger's old ladies again. The cats giggled.

"When are your people going, Sam?" asked Martha.

"Soon, I hope," said Sam. "They won't like being the only people left."

"Except the rag-and-bone man," Martha reminded him. "I suppose he doesn't really count because he never speaks to anyone. I don't believe he'll ever go."

"Well, if he doesn't, Pyewacket can come and stay with each of us in turn," said Pete. "Just imagine! Soon we'll each have a whole house to ourselves! I don't think there can be any other cats in the whole world who have houses all to themselves."

"I do wish they weren't taking down the fence," said Snowy in a worried voice. "And I don't care at all for the idea of a great big noisy factory just across the way."

"Look out!" exclaimed Pyewacket sharply. "Here comes another furniture van!"

The cats beat a hasty retreat as a second large van crawled past the one standing outside No. 2. It was a tight squeeze, and a good deal of shouting went on between the men. The second van came to a halt outside Sam's house.

The little girl opened the front door, stared wide-eyed at the van and then they heard her shout, "Ma! It's here!"

"What's here?" came her mother's voice from inside.

"The van!"

"My goodness! But it wasn't supposed to come until tomorrow! I'm not even half-packed!"

"Can't help that, ma'am," said one of the men. "If there's been a mistake it's not our fault; now that we're here we might as well get on with the job."

"Oh, very well," said the woman fretfully. "Beverley, you catch the cat."

"Puss, puss, puss!" shouted Beverley.

"Kitty – kitty – kitty!" called Ginger's old ladies down the lane.

Crash, hammer, bang went the two men who were taking down the fence. It was very noisy.

The cats melted away quietly and went back to the peace of Pyewacket's backyard.

By six o'clock that evening it was over. The furniture vans had gone, the workmen had gone, the mechanical monsters had been put away for the night and sat lumpily and silently on the now tidy and flattened vacant lot. The evening sunshine shone on the windows of the empty houses and on the sleek coats of the seven cats as they prowled around the deserted gardens, and delicately picked their way along the piled-up planks that had once been the high wooden fence.

"It does feel funny," said Pete uneasily. "It isn't a bit like I thought it was going to be."

"What's the matter with it?" demanded Pyewacket. "We've got what we wanted, haven't we?"

"Yes," said Pete. "Only—"

"I could do with a nice drop of milk," sighed old Snowy.

"Sometimes I had a tin of cat food for my supper," said Chi Ki reflectively. "The kind I liked best was called Pussycat Purr."

"Catch yourself a rat," said Pyewacket gruffly. "The Promise of Pan ended at four o'clock this afternoon."

"Can't be bothered," said Chi Ki. "I hate the taste of rat anyway, and I could just enjoy some Pussycat Purr."

He sighed deeply, and wandered off to the rag-and-bone man's yard. After a short pause all the other cats disappeared. Pete went home with Snowy. He said a whole empty house to himself gave him the creeps. Snowy caught a very small mouse which they shared for supper and they

washed it down with cold water from a puddle in the yard. None of the other cats fared much better, and that night all of them except Pyewacket had private thoughts about the wisdom of having frightened the humans away.

Early next morning, Martha was awakened by a peculiar noise on the roof of her house, which sounded like trampling feet. She ran downstairs and out through the broken window into the garden as fast as she could go. Looking up, she saw three men hard at work. Two of them were taking off the slates and throwing them down into the street below. The third man was attacking the chimney with a pickaxe. As she watched, the chimney fell with a crash, bricks flying in all directions. Martha was so startled that her fur stood up on end like a flue brush, and she arched her back and spat.

A wild screech from somewhere behind made her leap high in the air. She turned, claws out, teeth bared, to meet whatever danger threatened, and was just in time to see Pyewacket fall in the middle of the road, struck by a flying brick from the chimney! Blood trickled from a cut on his head and one back leg was clearly broken. He lay as still as if he was dead.

VIII *Up Goes the Factory*

Martha's heart missed a beat and then began to race. Pyewacket continued to lie quite still, his legs stretched out stiffly, his eyes closed. It had rained during the night, and his dark gray coat was wet and smeared with mud.

Martha crept closer and sniffed at his face. One ear, the torn one, twitched slightly and she felt a flood of relief. Pyewacket was still alive! But his head had been cut badly by the brick and he was still unconscious. Martha licked his nose gently. There seemed to be nothing more she could do.

The sound of footsteps made her start up, ready to fly at the first hint of danger. It was one of the workmen, and his face looked grave and kind.

" 'ello, kitty!" he said. "What's happened to your pal?" He looked around and his eye lighted on the brick, lying close to Pyewacket's head. "Why, the pore' old fellow!" he said, and then he shouted to his mate on the roof, "Hi! Bill! We've gone and killed a pore' old cat!"

"Don't you believe it!" shouted the man on the

roof. "You can't kill a cat. They've got nine lives!"

"Maybe he's had eight of 'em already!" the first man shouted back. Then he bent down and examined Pyewacket more closely. " 'Ang on a minute!" he called. "He's *not* dead. He twitched an ear! But he's got a broken leg."

Very gently, the man lifted Pyewacket and tucked him inside his coat. Then he shouted again to his mate on the roof. "I'll be back in ten minutes, Bill. He's hurt bad, and I'm taking 'im to the animal hospital!"

"Oh my goodness!" said Martha to herself. "Whatever will Pyewacket say to that when he comes to himself?"

"Poor old pussy," said the man gently and walked up Pig Lane toward the Market Square. Martha followed him a little way, but the busy traffic of the main street frightened her, and she stood, miserably uncertain, watching her leader being taken away. It was a terrible moment. At last, sadly, she went back down the lane to the rag-and-bone man's yard.

In the yard she found Pete. He had just killed a very small rat and was bursting with pride.

"Pete," she said soberly, "go and find all the others and tell them to come here."

86

"Can't," said Pete rather indistinctly because the rat was in his mouth. "I'm Pyewacket's messenger boy. I must stay here in case he wants me."

"He won't want you just now," Martha told him miserably. "Perhaps he will never want you again."

Pete's eyes nearly popped out of his head. He let the rat drop and whispered in a frightened voice, "Why not?"

"He's had a terrible accident," burst out Martha. "Oh Pete, do as I tell you! Go and find the others. This is more than I can bear alone!"

Silently, Pete ran out of the yard. He came back in a few minutes followed by Ginger and Sam. Snowy appeared from the pony's stable, and Chi Ki leaped gracefully down from the loft. Every face was grave and Pete was actually in tears.

In a few broken words, Martha told them what had happened. When she had finished, there was silence, except for Pete's desperate sobs.

"He—he may be all right," said Sam at last. "Pyewacket is very tough."

The old pony put his head over the stable door. It was still so early that the rag-and-bone man had not yet gone out to work.

"What's up?" he asked and, speaking all together, they told him.

"The animal hospital is a wonderful place," said the pony, looking kindly at the six unhappy cats. "I was there myself once when I fell down and broke my knees. If anyone can nurse Pyewacket back to health, they can."

"H-honestly?" gulped Pete.

"True as I stand here," said the pony. "I had the time of my life there. Pyewacket will soon be home again as good as new, you'll see."

This was comforting news, and soon the cats plucked up enough spirit to venture out of the yard into the lane, to see what was going on. The fence had now entirely disappeared and a whole army of men and machines were hard at work on the vacant lot. It was evident that, at long last, the factory was going to be built.

At ten o'clock, the men who were knocking down the houses stopped working and came down to the ground for their morning tea. They sat on the steps of No. 2, surrounded by broken slates and bits of brick, and sipped hot tea out of mugs.

Martha crept close to try and get news of Pyewacket, and sure enough she heard the nice man say, "That old cat's going to be all right.

88

The vet put three stitches in his head, and set the broken leg."

"Why bother?" said one of the other men carelessly. "He's only a stray."

"I'll bet he's a good ratter though," said the kind man. "This part of the town is alive with rats, they come up from the canal. That factory's going to need a good few cats about the place, to keep down the rats and mice."

"What is it they're going to make?" asked one of the other men. "Some kind of animal food isn't it? Dog biscuits?"

"No, cat food," said the kind man. "Pussycat Purr."

"*Never!*" thought Martha to herself in amazement and she scurried off to find the others and tell them the stupendous news.

"My, my!" said Chi when he heard what she had to say. "Now that really is something! I can put up with a factory opposite our houses if it's going to make Pussycat Purr."

"I don't know what you mean, 'opposite our houses'," said Ginger sourly. "Can't you see for yourself that our houses are being pulled down? And hasn't it occurred to any of you yet that this is why all the humans have moved out? It's had nothing to do with us at all!"

90

There was a long, long silence. The other five cats were so stunned by the knowledge that Ginger was, of course, right, that no one had anything to say. Then the same thought struck all of them, and they looked at each other, their furry faces wrinkled with worry and doubt.

Chi broke the silence at last.

"This will break Pyewacket's heart," he said, and the others murmured agreement.

"Oh, *poor* Pyewacket!" wailed Pete. "He thought he'd been so clever, and all the time—"

"So the rats didn't really help," remarked Martha thoughtfully. "We might just as well have been hunting them all this time. What a waste!"

"I can't help being glad it wasn't our doing that made my poor old man go into a home," said Snowy. "I've been feeling really bad these last few days."

"Now we know what the man in the bowler hat was doing," said Chi Ki. "Obviously he was telling them they had to go."

"And the big notice board," said Sam. "I'll bet that said the same thing."

"Wait a minute!" exclaimed Ginger. "I've just had a dreadful thought. If all our houses are being pulled down where are we going to live? Do you suppose the factory will be so huge that it will spread over the vacant lot *and* Pig Lane *and* all the space where the houses stand? Why, it would be enormous!"

"Factories are enormous," said Chi. "Just imagine all this ground being covered with tins and tins and tins of delicious Pussycat Purr."

"But where will we live?" asked Pete, and his voice trembled a little. "A cat's got to live somewhere. I wish Pyewacket was here. He'd tell us what to do."

"Who's going to tell Pyewacket that his wonderful plan has been a lot of nonsense?" asked Sam bluntly. "We ought to have had more sense, the whole bunch of us. How we could ever have believed that cats could drive people out of their homes—!"

"Cats *and* rats," Martha reminded him.

"Yes, but even so—" said Sam. "Pyewacket always did have big ideas. Why we listened to him I don't know. We would have done better to have moved with our people to their new homes. Now we've got no one to feed us, and very soon we won't even have a roof over our heads. We'll have to steal every mouthful of food, or else hunt, and one doesn't always feel in the mood for hunting. The whole thing is a mess, and I'm fed up!"

"Don't be so hateful, Sam," said Martha. "Poor

old Pyewacket is at death's door, and you talk about him that way."

Pete gave a loud wail. "He's not!" he cried. "He's not at death's door! Oh Snowy, say he's not! Martha, he isn't is he? Ginger—"

"*Do* be quiet, Pete," said Chi. "And you, Sam, you keep your big mouth shut too. Pyewacket is still our leader and if anyone talks against him they'll have to reckon with me. As to whether he's at death's door, we know he's not. Martha heard that nice man say he was going to be all right."

"Oh, so she did!" said Pete. "I'd forgotten. Isn't that *wonderful*?"

"So one day he'll come back, and someone is going to have to tell him the truth about his plan," said Sam. "Well, it's not going to be me."

"Selfish as usual," said Ginger.

Sam arched his back and his fur began to rise.

"Now boys, no fighting," begged old Snowy. "*I* will tell Pyewacket the truth."

"You'd be by far the best person," agreed Ginger, and all the others murmured agreement.

So that was arranged, and the cats settled down to wait for Pyewacket's return. Perhaps "settled down" is not quite the right expression, because from that day on it became harder and harder for the poor cats to lead any sort of settled life at all.

All day long, an army of workmen swarmed over the new factory site. The row of old houses in Pig Lane disappeared in a cloud of dust. They were so old that it took very little effort to bring them crashing down. One day they would stand there like doll's houses when the door is opened, with every room, upstairs and down, on full view from the street. The next day there would be nothing but a heap of rubble, and one of the huge mechanical monsters would pass over the ground, swallowing bricks like a great, house-eating dragon. Then the bulldozers followed, and left the place where the houses had been tidy and flat and ready for the builders to start all over again.

The factory rose rapidly, a palace of glass and concrete and steel. It covered the vacant lot and overflowed into Pig Lane. Where the houses had been, there was now a block of offices. When finally the rag-and-bone man, grumbling terribly, drove away with the pony and cart for the last time, the steel and glass buildings flowed over his yard too, and then there was nothing left of the old Pig Lane at all.

IX *Triumph of the Rats*

July that year was a cold, wet month, not a bit
like summer at all. The building site became a sea
of mud, which made the workmen grumble all
day, and the six homeless cats had an absolutely
miserable time. Only Pyewacket, snug in a warm
little bed in a cosy cage at the animal hospital, did
not suffer from the weather. His head felt a bit
queer, and one leg was in plaster, but for the first
time in his life he was comfortable and well-fed.
To his great surprise he found it enjoyable, even
though he was not free.

At first, he growled in his throat, and spat
viciously and tried to claw the hands of anyone
who came near him. But the vet and his assistant
were used to the ways of sick animals, and
handled him so gently and cleverly that somehow
he never managed to do them any harm.

What did surprise him was that they seemed to
bear him no grudge for trying to hurt them. He
was prepared to be kicked or clouted but, how-
ever badly he behaved, they remained gentle and

kind. When they went away and left him, he always felt more comfortable and knew that they had done him good.

"Come along Tiger, you old warrior," the vet would say as he lifted Pyewacket deftly out of his basket onto the table for treatment. The young girl stroked his head, very carefully because of the stitches, and called him "sweetie-pie". She brought him little bowls of warm milk in the morning and evening, and sometimes there would be fish for dinner, and sometimes "Pussycat Purr". Surrounded by all this kindness, Pyewacket began to have quite different ideas about life. He spent a lot of time just thinking things out and came to the conclusion that some humans weren't bad after all. When he was better, he intended to talk things over with the other six cats and exchange opinions. For the present though, he was quite content to lie in his comfortable basket, while his broken bone healed and the cut on his head became nothing more than a long, thin scar.

But for the other six cats life was not at all as comfortable as for Pyewacket, and they were very miserable. All through the day, the builders hammered and clanged and banged and shouted. Machines roared and rumbled, and the mud grew deeper and stickier, so that after even the shortest walk a cat had to spend hours cleaning his paws. At night it was quiet and would have been better, except for the rain. How it rained! They all crouched together under piles of timber and peered out at the teeming rain, too dispirited even to hunt, until sheer hunger drove them to action.

They began to wonder whether perhaps their misery was a punishment for being wicked enough to drive the humans out of their homes, and whether Pyewacket's dreadful accident was not a judgment on him for being their ringleader and working out the whole plot. The more they brooded about it, the more unhappy and guilty they felt, but it was too late now to make amends. Their families had all gone, and there was nothing left but mud and rain and noise.

The rats were giving trouble, too. They had become thoroughly out of hand during the time when they were protected by the Promise of Pan, and now they imagined themselves to be as good as any cat. They became perfect pests to the men working on the factory site, and were so fierce that the cats became too scared to tackle them. Poor old Snowy was badly bitten on the nose, and Pete limped for a week after a vicious nip on his paw. If Pyewacket had been there he would have rallied his forces and led them into battle against their ancient enemy. But with Pyewacket away the other six became cowed and spiritless, and lived on mice and beetles, leaving the rats to get on with their evil ways.

And what evil ways they were! Led by the chief rat, hoards of them came swarming up from the canal banks to the factory site. They stole the workmen's lunches almost under their very noses. They chewed holes in bags of cement – just for the fun of it – and worst of all, when the electricians began wiring the buildings for light and power, the rats chewed through the cables, so that all the work had to be done again.

The construction manager was furious! He sent for the town rat catcher, who called himself a Rodent Exterminator. This man set traps and put down poison, but only a few silly young rats got caught, and no one ate the poison because the chief rat knew all about it and warned them against it. Finally the rat catcher gave up in despair, and that very night a stupid young rat chewed through an electric cable which was "live". The rat was killed, but he had started a fire which burned down quite a large part of the factory. The six cats fled in terror as the bright flames lit up the sky and the fire engines came roaring to the building site. But the rats darted hither and thither screaming with joy, and some of the boldest even tried to chew a hole in one of the big, writhing hoses which carried water from the hydrants to put out the flames.

Next morning everyone on the site was gloomy and bad-tempered. The cats, creeping back to see what had happened, found one whole wing of the new factory blackened and burned, with twisted iron girders and shattered glass. One of the workmen threw a rock and hit Sam on the side of the head.

"Get out of here!" he yelled. "Thieving cats! Who stole my lunch yesterday, eh?"

"Not me," said Sam miserably, holding his aching head on one side. He went back to where the others were huddling under a crate and said, "We deserve it, you know. We've brought this on ourselves. If it hadn't been for us and the Promise of Pan, the rats would never have grown so bold, and now we're too scared to hunt them any more. What Pyewacket would think of us, I really shudder to think."

"Hush!" whispered Martha suddenly. "Keep still! Humans outside!"

The six cats huddled closer together under the old crate and tried not to breathe. If the workmen began blaming them for the invasion of the rats, there was no way of knowing what they might do to them in revenge.

Someone sat down heavily on the crate and gave a deep sigh. Then he spoke, and the cats recognized his voice. It was the manager, and he sounded tired and sad.

"This fire has been a terrible thing, George," he said. "It's set us back months, and I'll be blamed for it. A rat chewed through the wiring, that's what the fire brigade chiefs say. Why don't I have the rats kept down, that's what I'll be asked. Well, haven't I tried? The rat catcher tried just about everything. You know that, George, don't you?"

"Aye," came the voice of an old man.

"It's the night watchman," Sam whispered in Martha's ear. "The one with the kind face."

"Well, what more can I do?" asked the manager, and he sounded desperate.

"There's cats," said the old man slowly. "You want cats to keep down rats. That's the proper way of nature, that is."

"Bit old-fashioned, isn't it?" asked the manager doubtfully. "These new poisons were supposed to do the trick—"

"Only they didn't, did they?" said old George.

"Rats is too cunning by half. No, Mr. Hardy, sir. If I was you I'd try cats."

"All right, get hold of some," said the manager wearily. "Get as many as you can. You can draw rations for them from the .canteen."

"I'll do that," promised the old man. "There used to be a lot of cats around here at one time. Maybe they're still lurking around. Oh, and I know of a beauty if I can lay my hands on him. A regular, champion ratter, he is."

"I'll leave it to you then," said the other man, and he got up and slowly walked away.

George remained sitting on the crate. He took out his tobacco pouch and lit his ancient pipe. The smoke wafted through the slats of the crate and made Pete sneeze. It was only a very tiny sneeze but old George heard it, and bent his head. The frightened cats saw his face, almost as whiskery as theirs, peering in at them, and heard him give a chuckle of delight.

"So there you are, my beauties!" said the old man. "I knew you would be hanging around. What's the matter with you then that you don't have a go at the rats? Lost your spunk? Feeling sick? I can't see much of you in there, but I'm willing to bet that a nice drop of milk and a bit of warmth would put new heart into you. Come and see me tonight and I'll sign you on as members of the factory staff. Understand? Eight o'clock at the night watchman's hut, see?"

He got up, chuckling to himself at his own foolishness in making a date with cats, but little did he know how much of human language they understood. "Hut", "milk", "warmth", meant something to all of them.

As soon as it was dark the cats left the sanctuary of the old crate and made their way across the muddy ground to within a few yards of where a brazier burned inside a small, wooden hut. Beside the brazier sat the old man on a broken-backed chair, and he was frying sausages over the flames. On an upturned packing case by his side stood a bottle of milk, a bag of sugar and a tin mug. He leaned forward, his face ruddy in the firelight, and stirred the sausages with an old knife. A delicious smell arose and the six cats looked at one another, and licked their lips.

X   *The Cats Sign On*

Sam was the first cat to make a move. Very cautiously, he crept across the muddy ground to the open door of the little shed. Then he sat down and watched the old man, who was now heating water in a can for his tea. When he looked up, the old man saw Sam's great green eyes glittering in the dark.

"Hello, pussy!" he said. "So you've come, eh? Like a drop of milk?"

"You bet I would!" said Sam, and the old man seemed to understand, because he chuckled and poured some milk into a small jar that had held some kind of meat paste. It gave a delicious tang to the milk and Sam gulped it down greedily.

"Drop more?" asked the old man, looking at the milk bottle to see how much of it was left.

Sam began to purr and rub himself against the old man's legs. It was quite a treat, after all this time, to get a kind word from a human, and an even greater treat to be given milk. The old man poured out some more but, before Sam could start on it, the darkness around the hut became spangled with glittering eyes. Five pairs of anxious, hungry eyes appeared as the other cats, emboldened by Sam's success, left their hiding place and gathered around.

The night watchman looked at the six cats thoughtfully. He saw how thin they were, how wet and cold. He saw that Snowy was very old and Pete very young and that Chi Ki was not at all the sort of cat to be a stray. Sam and Ginger he decided could look after themselves, but Martha, he felt sure, was expecting babies and had no business to be out in the cold, wet night. He was a tender-hearted old man, very fond of cats, and he was thankful he had the manager's permission to give them good food and a job.

"Come on in, all of you," he said heartily. "Come on, don't be afraid of me. I'm just old George, the night watchman, and you're welcome to share my hut." He stooped down and picked up little Pete, who began to purr like a vacuum cleaner. Snowy rubbed her head lovingly against the old man's corduroy trousers and Martha, who knew only too well that the babies would soon be born, crept into the hut and sat down on a pile of sacks, her cold, pink feet kneading them as a baker kneads his dough. Sam, Ginger and Chi

Ki held back for a while, but Sam was sleepy after his delicious drink of milk, and when he settled down by the brazier Ginger and Chi Ki soon followed suit, blinking happily in the warmth of the glowing coals.

The old man looked again at the milk left in the bottle. Then he sighed a little and said to himself, "Oh well, tea without milk isn't so bad if you've plenty of sugar. I reckon I can do without milk for once."

He poured all the milk from the bottle into a little saucepan and warmed it over the fire. Then he poured it into a square tin box which had held his sandwiches and put it down on the floor.

"Room for all of you round that," he said. "All but you, old friend," and he picked up Sam. "Fair do's. You've had your share. Come on now, the rest of you – dig in!"

Never had warm milk tasted so good! None of the six cats had eaten anything except rats and mice and stuff out of garbage cans since their owners had gone away. They drank every drop and then licked the driblets off their whiskers and paws. The old man ate his sausages, throwing each of them little bits in turn. It was a gorgeous midnight feast.

"If only Pyewacket was here!" sighed Martha, but the others wondered uneasily whether he would consider them traitors for making friends with a human.

"Now I'll tell you what," said old George when the meal was finished to the last crumb and drop. "We need the whole gang of you here. If you've been hanging around, and I've a pretty good idea that you have, then you ought to be ashamed of yourselves for letting the rats get so bold."

The cats shifted uncomfortably and avoided the old man's eyes. They knew very well that they had behaved in a lazy and cowardly fashion, though it was hard to admit this, even to themselves.

"Can't see that it was our job to hunt rats for strangers," muttered Ginger to Sam. "It was different when our own people lived in Pig Lane."

"Yes, perhaps there's something in that," admitted Sam. "Still, it's a matter of pride with cats, to keep the upper hand."

"We've been to blame," said Chi Ki decidedly. "Without our leader we all went to pieces."

"It's been so dreadfully cold and wet," sighed old Snowy. "It takes the heart out of you to have no owner and no home."

"You should have thought of that when Pyewacket first suggested his great plan," put in Martha sharply.

"I did, dear," said Snowy. "I thought about it a lot, but what could I do when my poor old man went away?"

"It's been worse for me than for any of you," grumbled Martha. "I've been worried to death about what to do with my babies when they come."

"If we all catch rats that man said they'd feed us," said little Pete hopefully. "I didn't mind my people going away because I hated that boy, and while Pyewacket was around everything was fun, but since then it's been horrible. I've felt too weak to go ratting and nobody loves me—"

"Don't be such a baby!" said Ginger sharply. "That man's looking at you. You mustn't cry."

Pete shut his small pink mouth and gulped. It was true, he had been about to give a real, heartbroken yowl.

"Poor old pussies," said old George. "You've had a bad time, haven't you? But it's over now. The manager told me to find cats, and cats I've found. Tomorrow I'll get you signed on as members of the staff and then you'll get your rations regular. Mind you, you'll have to work for your living. As soon as the building is finished, the fish will be arriving for Pussycat Purr, boxes and boxes of it every day. If the rats are a nuisance now just think what they'll be like then! We'll feed you up properly. Then you'll get your courage back and you can clear 'em all out easily. Clean sweep, eh? You can do it if you really try."

"Of course we can!" said Chi Ki, speaking for them all. The night watchman nodded kindly and left the hut to go on his rounds of the factory site. As soon as he had gone the six of them gathered closer around the brazier and burst into eager talk.

"My word!" said Sam. "Talk about luck!"

"Official Rodent Exterminators to Pussycat Purr," said Chi Ki. "Sounds good to me."

"What's a Rodent Extermin – er – what you said?" inquired Pete. "I thought we just had to catch rats."

"It's the same thing, dear," Snowy told him. "It's just a grand name for a rat catcher."

"I'm going to have a grand name!" yelled Pete. "Ginger, did you hear that? I'm a Rodent Extermater! Martha, I'm a Rodent Examater! Sam, I'm a—"

"Shut up," said Sam, and Pete subsided, muttering happily to himself," Rodent extra-terminator, that's me."

"I wonder what the rations will be?" said Ginger. "If only these people talked cat language we could make terms with them. It gives one a sort of frustrated feeling when they're all so stupid. Personally, I think we ought to hold out for half a pint of milk each and a tin of Pussycat Purr every day."

"You don't think they'll expect us to eat rat, do you?" asked Chi Ki distastefully. "I simply can't. I don't mind hunting for sport, but I really can't eat the creatures."

"I can," said Ginger, "if there isn't anything else."

"Dear old chap, I don't mean to be offensive, but Siamese are rather different from the – er – common run, aren't they?" said Chi Ki. Ginger bristled and got up, stiff-legged.

"Now boys, no fighting," said Snowy hastily. "I feel quite sure we shall be well fed. If they give their night watchman those lovely sausages when all he has to do is to sit by a fire, then I'm quite sure the official rat catchers will live off the fat of the land. And after all they make cat food here. It won't cost them a penny to hand out some of it to us."

"We can always go on strike if they don't," said Sam. "My master was always going on strike.

And there's one thing I do think we ought to agree on. If we take this job we remain our own bosses. We work here, but we belong to ourselves, not to them. Cats don't need owners in the way dogs do. Food and comfort, yes, but a lot of mushy affection, no."

"Would you say that?" inquired Snowy doubtfully. "I was very fond of my dear old man."

"We'll make an exception for you," suggested Sam. "You can be fond of the night watchman, but the rest of us will just stay independent. Agreed?"

"Agreed!" said Ginger, Chi Ki and Pete. Martha did not join in, and when they looked for her they found she was no longer there.

"Where's she gone?" demanded Sam crossly, but old Snowy smiled wisely.

"Leave her alone," she said. "And now, boys, if you really want to earn your keep I suggest you start working right away. I've just seen two rats peeping at us around that concrete mixer, and there's another one on top of the pile of bricks."

As the four cats melted away into the darkness, Snowy tiptoed over to the back of the shed where a pile of sacks made a soft and comfortable bed.

"Martha," she whispered, "are you all right?"

There was no reply, but when Snowy peeped cautiously into the corner she saw Martha con-

tentedly asleep. Curled up in the warmth of her
flank, there were five fat little kittens, two blacks,
one white and two grays.

"The darlings!" whispered Snowy sentiment-
ally, and at that moment the night watchman
came back from his rounds. He looked for the cats
and, seeing only Snowy, shone his torch into the
corner where she stood. When he saw Martha and
her family, his wrinkled face softened and he
smiled delightedly.

"Five more Rodent Exterminators!" he said.
"That makes eleven. I'll have a word with the
manager first thing in the morning and sign 'em
all on. Eleven good cats, that's fine. But I wonder
what happened to that big gray tom that belonged
to the rag-and-bone man? Now there was a
champion ratter if ever there was one. I'd give a
lot to have him on the staff."

Snowy listened to this wide-eyed. Then she
slipped out of the night watchman's hut and made
her way through the rain. She went across the
now empty, silent Market Square and down the
main shopping street until she reached the animal
hospital on the other side of the town. Jumping
up lightly onto the wall which surrounded a yard
full of kennels and pens she sat down and raised
her voice.

"Pyewacket!" she called. "Pye-wacket! Pye-wack-*et*!"

"Drat that yowling cat," People murmured sleepily from the houses nearby, but inside the animal hospital Pyewacket stirred and woke.

XI *The Round Dozen*

When Snowy got back to the night watchman's hut the dawn was breaking, the fire in the brazier had almost burned itself out, and the old man himself was preparing to go home for a good day's sleep. Sam, Ginger, Chi Ki and Pete, looking tired but happy, were sitting around resting after a strenuous rat hunt which had resulted in a bag of twelve rats and (Pete's contribution) quite a large mouse. From the pile of sacks in the corner came little squeaks and movements and the sound of Martha starting on the morning baths. They heard her rough little tongue busily at work on the tiny, squirming kittens.

The old watchman took some milk before he left and put it in a saucer by Martha's side. Then he looked at the rest of the cats and gave them a friendly nod.

"See you tonight," he said. "Eight o'clock I come on duty, so be sure you're all here. I'll have a word with the manager about you as soon as I can. He'll be glad to sign you on, so don't worry about that. 'Morning all." And he went away to his home in the town.

As soon as he had gone, the cats turned to Snowy, eager for news.

"Well?" they said. "Did you see him?"

"See who?" asked Snowy, just to tease.

"Oh, don't pretend!" said Ginger. "We know where you went off to last night. Did you find Pyewacket?"

Snowy arched her back and yawned. Then she stood on her hind legs and began to sharpen her claws against the rough wooden walls of the hut. She was dying to tell her news, and yet it was fun to keep the others waiting just for a bit.

"Come on, Snowy!" begged Chi Ki.

Snowy sat down and began to lick her feet.

"Yes, I saw him," she said. "He sent his kind regards to all of you and congratulations to Martha. He says if there's a boy he'd like it called after him."

"There are three boys," said Martha proudly. "But not one of them is going to have an outlandish name like Pyewacket. I'm going to call them – er – er – well, I'll have to think."

"I wouldn't mind being called Pyewacket," said Pete. "I'd be proud. How is he, Snowy? When's he coming out?"

"Well, that's just it," said Snowy. "He's almost well. They took the plaster off his leg yesterday and he only limps a tiny bit. But they plan to find him a good home with a nice, respectable family—"

Sam gave a screech of laughter.

"Pyewacket in a respectable home!" he said. "That's a joke, that is!"

"Don't they know he's always lived with the rag-and-bone man?" demanded Chi Ki. "Mind you, I'm not saying a word against Pyewacket, but he'd never fit into a respectable home."

"He'd run away," said Pete.

"Well, of course he would," Snowy assured them. "But the thing is, you see, he'd have to go there because he's shut inside a cage and he can't get out. So we talked it all over and I told him about our new job—"

"Does he approve?" asked Martha from her corner. "Does he want to join the firm?"

"Yes, I think he does. Of course he'd want to be Chief Rodent Exterminator but none of us mind that, do we?"

There was a short silence. Then Sam said, "Not much good minding. Pyewacket always has been boss and he always will be. Anyway, he's twice as smart as any of us and we can trust him to stand up for our rights."

"But if he's locked in a cage how's he going to get here?" asked Pete anxiously. "Oh, I do want to see him again! Ginger, don't you want to see Pyewacket? Chi, don't you—"

"Shut up," said Chi Ki. "How is he going to escape, Snowy?"

"Quite simple," said Snowy. "He'll let them take him to the new home and then, first chance he gets, he'll just walk out and come here."

"Suppose they butter his paws?" asked Martha. "That's magic, to make a cat settle down."

"Pyewacket's magic is stronger than butter," Snowy assured her. "He'll be along in a day or two, you'll see."

That night, when the old watchman came on duty at eight o'clock, all the cats were lined up by his little hut to greet him. They were delighted to see that he had three bottles of milk under his arm and in his hand he carried a string bag almost bursting with tins of Pussycat Purr.

"Hello mates," he said cheerily as he put down his burdens on the packing case in the hut. "All here, are you? And how's the family?" He peered into the corner where Martha lay contentedly with the five babies closely cuddled up, and a slow smile creased his kind old face.

"Little darlings!" he said. Martha began to purr.

From one of the large pockets of his old coat the watchman brought out a stack of tin dishes. He filled six of them with generous helpings of Pussycat Purr and then lined them up on the floor.

"Rations," he said. "Come and get it, all of you. Come along mother, leave the babies for a bit, you must have a break sometimes."

Martha got up carefully and the babies rolled over into the middle of the nest she had made in the sacks. One gave a loud squeak and Martha paused anxiously, but it dropped off to sleep again and she joined the others at their meal.

"Well, it's all in order," said the old man, watching them eat. "I saw the manager today and he gave me permission to sign on twelve cats. I'm to be in charge of you, and your rations will be a third of a pint of milk each and one tin of Pussycat Purr. For that you'll be expected to put in a good night's work and show results. In the daytime you're off duty and can do what you like, but you're welcome to sleep in here. 'Course, when the factory is finished I'll have a proper night watchman's office in the building, with a real fireplace and everything comfy and nice. And I'll share it with you, all twelve of you."

The cats looked at each other in a puzzled sort of way and began to add up in their heads.

"There's me," thought Chi Ki. "That's one. And Sam, two. Ginger, three. Snowy, four. Martha, five. Little Pete, six. And five kittens makes eleven." Chi Ki was very good at arithmetic for a cat. "Now eleven isn't twelve, so either the old man can't count or else he's got something up his sleeve."

"If the old man has signed on another cat it's going to be dreadfully awkward," thought Snowy. "Pyewacket may turn up any time now and if he's not needed here whatever will he do? Anyway, none of us will want to stay without him. Oh dear, what *shall* we do?"

Sam and Ginger were still trying to work out the number in their heads. Twice Sam went over to the corner and counted the kittens, thinking that perhaps there were only four – or would it be six? He was in a real muddle and felt his head whirling.

Only Pete was happy. He couldn't count at all and was perfectly sure that everything was going to be all right.

The old man put his kettle on the brazier to boil water for a cup of tea before starting on his rounds. He talked aloud to the cats because he was lonely and had the feeling that they could understand.

"Six grown cats and five kittens makes eleven," he said. "Bet you're wondering why I said twelve?" He put the tea in the pot and opened a bottle of milk. "What about a little drink, eh? Have half your milk now and the rest later on in the night. You'll be glad to have it after a few hours' hunting, I don't doubt."

He poured milk into the six tin dishes and all the cats drank, but their feeling of uneasiness grew and grew.

"Twelve cats I've got permission to sign on," said the old man. "Eleven cats I've got. So we want one more, eh? Well, I've got one, and a real good one, too!"

Each cat's heart sank into its paws. Here was bad news indeed! A strange cat to be brought into their midst instead of their leader, their intrepid leader, the great Pyewacket! How could they bear it? And yet, how could they give up this glorious job with its promise of good food and shelter for the rest of their lives? But Snowy had assured Pyewacket that they were all waiting for his return. How could they possibly say, "Sorry, Pyewacket. *We're* all right, but there's no place here for you"?

It couldn't be done. When the new cat arrived, they would have to go. Even Martha would have to carry her new-born babies, one by one, to another place. No more milk, no more Pussycat Purr, no friendly night watchman and his lovely warm fire, nothing but the wet streets, the un-friendly dogs, the garbage cans. It was a bleak prospect, but to their great credit not one cat faltered. Loyalty to their leader came first. If it was a choice between Pyewacket and Pussycat Purr, then Pyewacket it would be.

Footsteps were heard, coming across the open space in front of the half-built factory. They were the firm, loud footsteps of someone who has a right to be there and the night watchman got up and went out of the hut to see who it was.

"Hello," the cats heard him say. "It's you, eh? You've brought him then?"

"Yes, I've brought him," said a man's voice and the six cats looked at each other in despair. The terrible moment had arrived sooner than they expected. The twelfth cat was here!

"Bring him in then," said old George, and he came back into the hut, followed by a young man carrying a covered basket. The basket seemed to be jumping about with a life of its own, and very angry noises came from inside.

"My word, it's not half in a state," chuckled the old man. "Let 'im out."

"You don't think he'll go for the others?" asked the young man doubtfully. "He's all right with me, but he was very wild at first, and I don't know what he'll be like when I let him loose."

"The others will have to take their chance," said old George. "They're good cats, all of them, but that one you've got there, he's a winner. I know him of old. Worth all the rest put together as a ratter, he is."

"Well *really!*" exclaimed Chi indignantly. "As if everyone didn't know that Pyewacket is champion ratter in this town. I say nothing about the insult to us, but if this cat thinks he's going to boss us around he'll find out his mistake soon enough."

"We'll all walk out," Ginger assured him. The basket gave a violent bound.

Very cautiously, the young man undid the straps and lifted the lid. The six cats stood around, tense and bristling, ready to fight, if necessary. Martha kept glancing anxiously at her kittens as if she was afraid the strange cat would gobble them up. Snowy was nearly in tears because it was she who had promised their leader that there was a place waiting for him.

A head came out of the basket, a gray head, with a torn ear and a long, white scar down one side of the face. One great green eye and one which was half-closed, surveyed the circle of cats and the kindly face of old George. Then white teeth parted in a friendly grin.

It was Pyewacket himself!

Printed in Great Britain by C. Tinling & Co.,
Liverpool, London and Prescot